Daniel O'Dowd was ever so loud

by Julie Fulton

Illustrated by

Elina Ellis

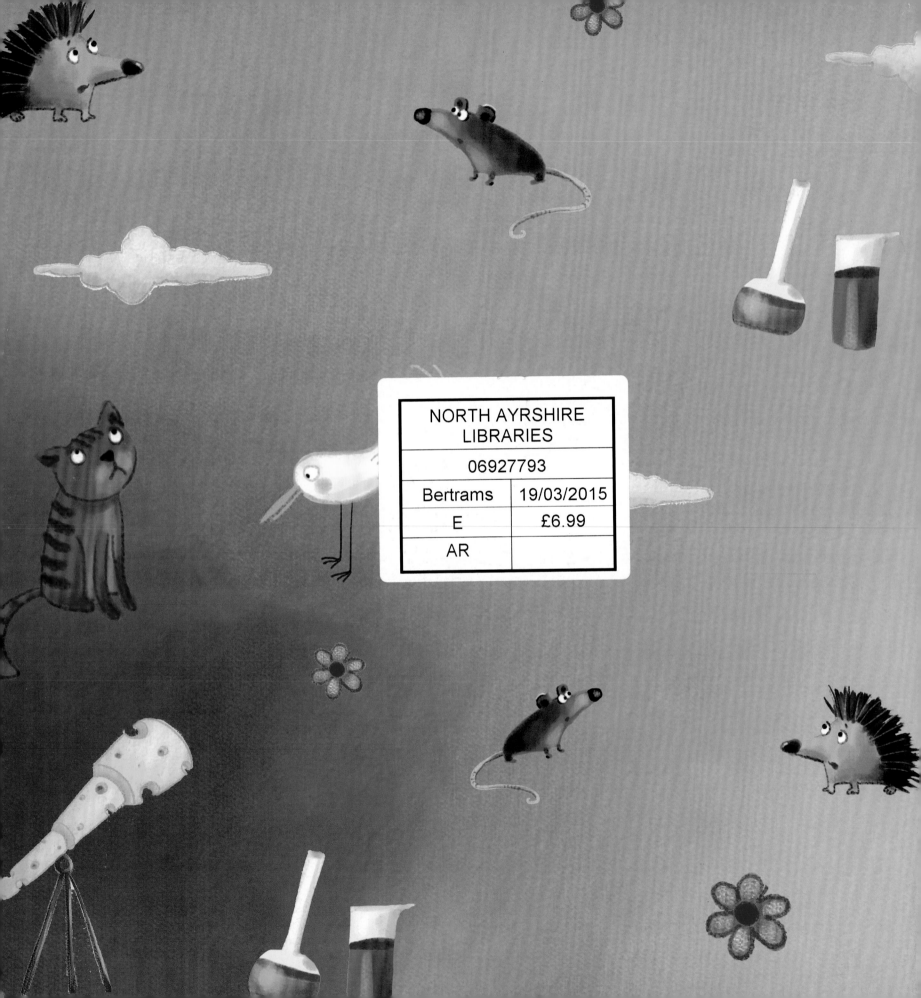

Daniel O'Dowd was **ever** so loud.
He shouted wherever he went.
At the zoo the chimps **cried** when his mouth opened **wide**
and the elephant hid in a tent.

When he shouted at school, his teacher, Miss Pool,
wrapped a **big** woolly scarf round her head.
She declared, "I've no doubt, if you **stopped** shouting out,
you would hear something useful instead."

The class went to visit Professor McWhizzit.
He built things like airports for bees,
mad machines to cut hair, an invisible chair
and a telescope made out of cheese.

OPEN DAY!

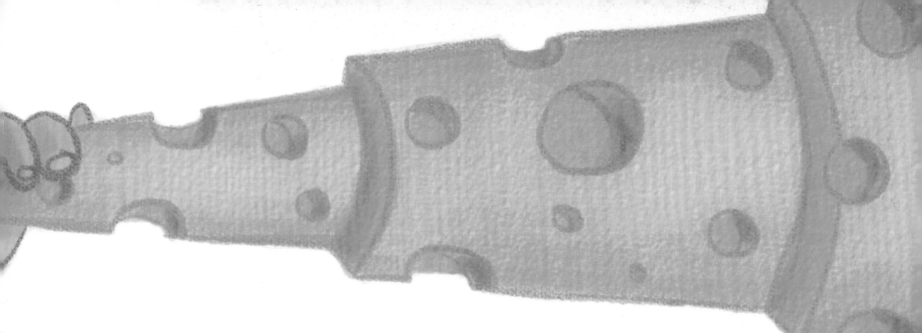

Daniel shouted, "**Yippee!** Let me look, let me see!"
All the noise made Miss Pool start to frown.
Daniel's shouts grew **SO** loud they scared all the crowd
and made the town's lighthouse fall down.

Daniel **screwed** up his face and looked up into space.
He saw satellites, planets and stars.
Then he shouted in shock, "I can see a **huge** rock
and it's racing towards us from Mars!"

Professor McWhizzit said, "Hang on a minute!
I've a **rocket** I made from a clock.
If I send Daniel out and he gives a big shout,
I think he could **shatter** the rock!"

Daniel clambered on board, the engines all **roared**
and the rocket shot way, way up high.
It **zoomed** past the moon and a spaceship and soon
it was next to the rock in the sky.

Daniel gave a loud shout, the noise echoed about,
but the rock simply **shuddered** and **twitched.**
So he shouted lots more, more than ever before,
and.........

BANG!

the rock burst into bits.

The Professor said, "**WOW!** You can stop shouting now.
I'll explain how to fly back to Earth."

But the boy didn't hear what was said in his ear - he was **cheering** for all he was worth.

The rocket sped on and soon it had gone

many miles from young Daniel's home town.

When he saw with a **fright** the earth vanish from sight

Daniel cried out, "I want to get down!"

He bellowed and yowled, he hollered and howled,
till his face went a bright rosy red.
Then he thought of Miss Pool and her **listening rule**.
"I mustn't shout, I must listen instead."

The Professor cried, "**Quick!** Pull the red control stick."

Daniel pulled it as hard as he could.

The rocket swung round and flew back to the **ground**,

landing right where the lighthouse had stood.

Daniel O'Dowd was no longer so loud.

His adventure had made it quite plain.

"I will **listen** lots more, I won't shout like before...

...unless Earth needs **saving** again!"

The End
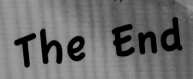

Daniel O'Dowd was ever so loud
is an original concept by
© Julie Fulton

Illustrator: Elina Ellis
Represented by Advocate Art

Published by MAVERICK ARTS PUBLISHING LTD
Studio 3A, City Business Centre, 6 Brighton Road,
Horsham, West Sussex, RH13 5BB
© Maverick Arts Publishing Limited January 2015 +44 (0)1403 256941

A CIP catalogue record for this book is available at the British Library.

ISBN 978-1-84886-118-3

Maverick
arts publishing
www.maverickbooks.co.uk